WHO SAID RED?

WHO SAID RED?

Mary Serfozo

illustrated by Keiko Narahashi

Aladdin Paperbacks

To Dana, Sara, Jonathan, and Aaron
M.S.

For Peter and Micah
K.N.

First Aladdin Paperbacks edition 1992

Text copyright © 1988 by Mary Serfozo
Illustrations copyright © 1988 by Keiko Narahashi

Aladdin Paperbacks
An imprint of Simon & Schuster Children's Publishing Division
1230 Avenue of the Americas
New York, NY 10020

Printed in Hong Kong
10 9 8 7 6 5 4

Library of Congress Cataloging-in-Publication Data
Serfozo, Mary.
    Who said red? / Mary Serfozo ; illustrated by Keiko Narahashi. —
1st Aladdin Books ed.
       p.   cm.
    Summary: A little girl and her brother introduce red, green, blue,
yellow, and other colors as they wander about their farm.
    ISBN 0-689-71592-7
    [1. Color—Fiction.   2. Stories in rhyme.]   I. Narahashi, Keiko,
ill.   II. Title.
PZ8.3.S4688wh   1992
[E]—dc20   91-21160

Who said red?

Did you say red?
A Santa red,
A stop sign red,

A cherry, berry, very red.

Did you say red?

YES, I SAID RED!

You don't mean green?
Look, here is green....

A pickle green,
A big frog green,

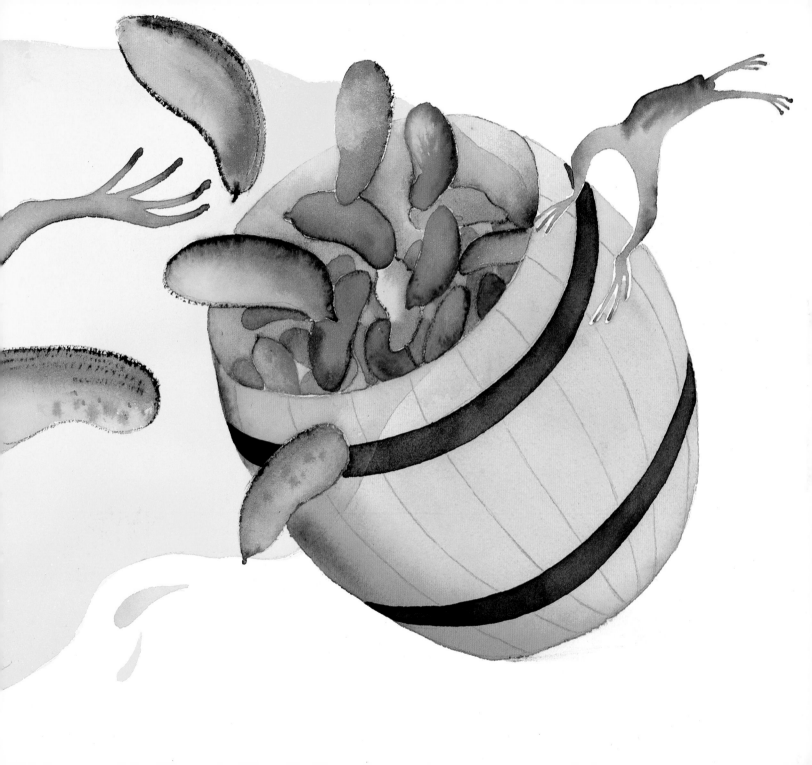

A leaf, a tree,
a green bean green.

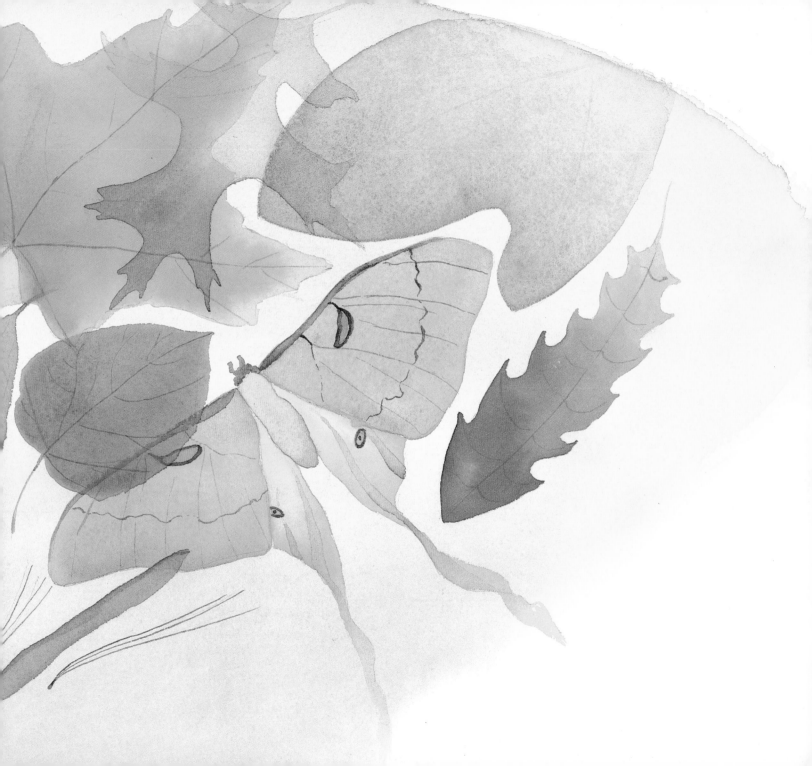

Did you say green?

NO, I SAID RED!

Now who said blue?
Could it be you?

A blue sky blue,
A blue eye blue,

A bow, a ball, a blue jean blue.

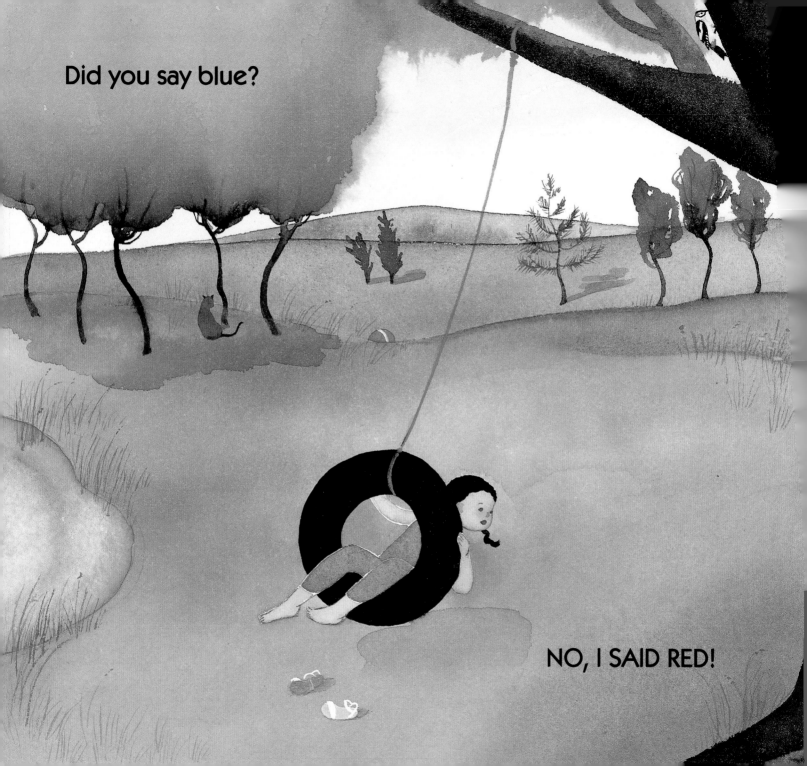

Did you say blue?

NO, I SAID RED!

Well hello, yellow....
Bright and mellow.

Slicker yellow,
Sunshine yellow,

Lemonade and daisy yellow.

Not purple, then,
Or brown or pink…

Not orange, or black
Or white, I think.

Tell me, again,
Just what you said.

Did you say red?

YES, I SAID RED!